Some mornings when Ben
wakes up he's a **wild wolf.**

Or a knight.

Or a **monster** covered in scars.
He paints them on his face with Anna's make-up.
Anna is his big sister. Ben always makes sure he
creeps into her room as quietly as a spider.

But sometimes he's not quiet enough . . .
and then Anna tickles him.

Big sisters know
exactly where little
brothers are ticklish.
Luckily, she doesn't
catch him too often.

Ben loves to paint big bloodstains on Anna's desk with her lipstick.

He tells her they're from a man-eating monster,
who especially likes to eat girls . . .
and that he'll protect her.

Then Anna hides in the wardrobe
and makes monster noises.
She's very good at those.
She **grunts**
and **snorts**
and **growls**.

And Ben, strong
as an elephant
and brave as a lion,

fetches his three
plastic swords and
the water pistol as big
as a pumpkin,

and fights until
he's red in the face

and the man-eating
monster doesn't utter
the smallest squeak.

On Mondays,
Wednesdays and
Fridays he fights the
three grisly green
ghouls howling in
the bathroom.

Anna's really
scared of them.

But Ben slashes them to ribbons and flushes them down the toilet.

O n Tuesdays and Thursdays
he deals with the slime-burping beastie
that loves to lick out the kitchen pans.

Ben usually throws the beastie from the balcony, though it always leaves slime on his hands. But that's the only way to get rid of it.

The Saturday-burglar, Ben lassos with Anna's skipping rope. That works really well.

Though when the burglar fights back really hard, sometimes some of Anna's posters get knocked off the wall.

But Ben makes up for it by
protecting Anna from foxes
and wolves, when she's picking
dandelion leaves for the
guinea pigs in the garden.

Or he keeps an eye on the bears
that lurk among the trees, just waiting
to gobble up his tasty big sister.

Yes it's true, Ben fights a lot.
All week long in fact.
It's hard work protecting Anna.

But in the evening,
when Night presses
her soot black face
against his window
and the heating rattles
like a thousand biting beetles,
Ben crawls into Anna's bed . . .

. . . and it feels so good to have a
big sister to protect him, for a change.

First published in Germany by Verlag Friedrich Oetinger, Hamburg © 2004

This edition first published in the United Kingdom in 2006 by
The Chicken House, 2 Palmer Street, Frome, Somerset, BA11 1DS
www.doublecluck.com
Paperback edition first published in 2008

Printed and bound in China by Imago

British Library Cataloguing in Publication Data available
Library of Congress Cataloguing in Publication data available
978-1-905294-66-4